Cornflakes

MW00906074

It was breakfast time.

The bears ate cornflakes.

They gave two cornflakes

to their pet mouse Squeak.

"Squeak loves cornflakes,"
said Little Bear.
Then he said, "Oh dear!
Cat is at the door!"

"We must hide Squeak!"
Big Bear said to Little Bear,
and he put the mouse
in the cornflakes box.

"Hello, Bears," said Cat.
"I have run out of milk.
Please, may I have
a cup of milk?"

Cat bent over the table.
She looked at the cornflakes.
"What is that squeaky noise?"
she said to the bears.

"Cornflakes!" said Little Bear.
"Some cornflakes go crackle.
Some cornflakes go pop.
Our cornflakes go squeak."

When Cat left, Big Bear said,
"Get Squeak out of the cornflakes."
Little Bear tipped up the box.
"What cornflakes?" he said.